S0-CYF-179

GRANDPAS
Are the
Greatest

For Arthur and Norman —B. F.

For Tom —N. T.

BLOOMSBURY CHILDREN'S BOOKS
Bloomsbury Publishing Inc., part of Bloomsbury Publishing Plc
1385 Broadway, New York, NY 10018

BLOOMSBURY, BLOOMSBURY CHILDREN'S BOOKS, and the Diana logo
are trademarks of Bloomsbury Publishing Plc

First published in Great Britain as *Grandads Are the Greatest* in May 2023 by Bloomsbury Publishing Plc
Published in the United States of America in May 2023
by Bloomsbury Children's Books

Text copyright © 2023 by Ben Faulks
Illustrations copyright © 2023 by Nina Tudor

All rights reserved. No part of this publication may be reproduced or transmitted in any form or by any means, electronic or mechanical,
including photocopying, recording, or any information storage or retrieval system, without prior permission in writing from the publisher.

Bloomsbury books may be purchased for business or promotional use. For information on bulk purchases please contact
Macmillan Corporate and Premium Sales Department at specialmarkets@macmillan.com

Library of Congress Cataloging-in-Publication Data
available upon request
ISBN 978-1-5476-1230-7 (hardcover) • ISBN 978-1-5476-1231-4 (e-book) • ISBN 978-1-5476-1232-1 (ePDF)

Book design by Goldy Broad
Typeset in Caroni Avenue
Printed and bound in China by Leo Paper Products, Heshan, Guangdong
2 4 6 8 10 9 7 5 3 1

To find out more about our authors and books visit www.bloomsbury.com and sign up for our newsletters.

GRANDPAS
Are the
Greatest

Ben Faulks

Nia Tudor

BLOOMSBURY
CHILDREN'S BOOKS
NEW YORK LONDON OXFORD NEW DELHI SYDNEY

GRANDPAS'
SUMMER PICNIC

"Grandpa! Grandpa! Grandpa!
Will you sit me on your knee?
Tell me, did you have a grandpa,
when you were small like me?"

"Of course, I did—and just like you,
he had a **grandpa** too!
There's a great long line of grandpas
that leads all the way to **you**.

Now, every grandpa's different
in shape and size and name.
Look around and you will see—
no two are quite the same."

"My grandpa is a BAKER
and is famous for his cakes.
He's taught me all his secrets . . .

LOOK what I can make!"

"My grandpa is a BUILDER,
who's built a **hundred** homes.
And now that he's retired . . .

I've got
one of **my own.**"

"My grandpa's an EXPLORER,
who's traveled everywhere!

And once when I went with him,
we met a grizzly bear."

"My grandpa's an INVENTOR.
He's made me lots of things:
like an automatic paintbrush,

and popcorn-powered wings!"

"My grandpa is a BARBER,
and has a crazy beard.
He's had all sorts of haircuts . . .

that are
wonderful and weird."

"My grandpa is a FISHERMAN.
He tells me salty tales . . .
of sea monsters and mermaids,
megalodons and whales."

"My grandpa's a MAGICIAN who tours across the land . . .

and I'm his young apprentice,
who lends a **helping** hand."

"My grandpa has a head for HEIGHTS—
he hang-glides through the sky.
Nothing makes me happier
than when we get to fly."

"My grandpa *doesn't* hang-glide
or sail the seven seas,
but he's the kind of grandpa
who **stays** at home with **me**.

You read me books and sing me songs . . .

And wrap me up
in **cuddles**.

You're **always** there to
help me out if I get
in a **muddle**."

"Well, my grandpa
did the same for me:
he loved me through
and through . . .

And now that you're my grandchild,
I'll do the same for
YOU."

"So, here's to ALL the grandpas,
whatever lives they live.
You can **always** count on grandpas . . .

. . . for the LOVE they have
to give."